This one's for
Lizzy, Lucia, Ona, Ezra and Julian
—P.B.

For Madiba, a lifelong hero.
And for my dad, Richard Jesse Watson,
who taught me how to work
—J.J.W.

G. P. PUTNAM'S SONS
Published by the Penguin Group
Penguin Group (USA) LLC
375 Hudson Street, New York, NY 10014

USA | Canada | UK | Ireland | Australia
New Zealand | India | South Africa | China
penguin.com
A Penguin Random House Company

Library of Congress Cataloging-in-Publication Data
Bildner, Phil.
The soccer fence / by Phil Bildner ; illustrated by Jesse Joshua Watson.
pages cm
Summary: Each time Hector watches white boys playing soccer in Johannesburg, South Africa, he dreams of playing on a real pitch one day, and after the fall of apartheid, when he sees the 1996 African Cup of Nations team, he knows that his dream can come true.
Includes historical note, sources, and timeline of apartheid.
[1. Soccer—Fiction. 2. Apartheid—Fiction. 3. Race relations—Fiction. 4. Blacks—South Africa—Fiction. 5. Johannesburg (South Africa)—History—20th century—Fiction. 6. South Africa—History—1961–1994—Fiction. 7. South Africa—History—1994—Fiction.] I. Watson, Jesse Joshua, illustrator. II. Title.
PZ7.B4923Soc 2014 [E]—dc23 2013014675
Manufactured in China by RR Donnelley Asia Printing Solutions Ltd.
ISBN 978-0-399-24790-3
10 9 8 7 6 5

Design by Ryan Thomann. Text set in Aptifer Slab. The line art was done in pencil and processed digitally, then painted in acrylic on illustration board.
The publisher does not have any control over and does not assume any responsibility for third-party websites or their content.

THE Soccer Fence

A STORY OF FRIENDSHIP, HOPE AND APARTHEID IN SOUTH AFRICA

PHIL BILDNER

illustrated by **JESSE JOSHUA WATSON**

G. P. PUTNAM'S SONS · AN IMPRINT OF PENGUIN GROUP (USA)

I kicked the egg-shaped ball toward the goal.

"He shoots!" I shouted.

The ball soared past my sister's fingertips, just inside the leaning stack of empty cartons.

"Goooaaalll!"

With my fist in the air, I sprinted up the field along the wire fence, the out-of-bounds that separated our Johannesburg township from the rest of the world.

Twice a month, my sister and me rode the PUTCO bus with Mama.
She took us to a different part of Johannesburg where she worked.

"Stay out of trouble," Mama always warned as she led us to the yard.

My sister usually spent all day in the garden, trimming and
raking and planting and smiling. I spent all day with my face pressed
to the fence, my eyes glued to the boys chasing after the black-and-
white leather ball.

"Hey!" I called. "Hey!"

But not a single boy ever looked my way as they raced up and back
along the green carpet.

"One day," I whispered, "I'm going to play on a field just like that.
One day real soon."

"Today, we celebrate liberty!"
Papa raised his hands to the heavens.

Nelson Mandela had been freed from prison. Apartheid had finally crumbled.

We paraded to FNB Stadium with the other families from our township.

High in the packed upper deck, we waved flags, danced in the aisles and listened to our hero.

"We are going forward," Nelson Mandela declared. "The march towards freedom and justice is irreversible."

But the march was slow.

The next time I went to work with Mama,

I peeked over the fence.

"Can I play?" I called.

Not a single boy looked my way.

Then one time, a couple of years later while I was helping my sister in the garden, their ball sailed over the fence.

"I'll get it!" I shouted.

I chased it down and bicycle-kicked it high into the air and back over the fence, right to the blond boy standing by midfield. He trapped my pass with his foot and booted the ball onto the field.

Then he turned away and rejoined his game.

"Today, we celebrate liberty!" Papa raised his hands to the heavens.

For the first time ever, people of all races could vote in South Africa.

We stood for hours and hours in the snaking line at the polling station. When Papa finally cast his ballot, he hugged me tighter than he ever had.

A few days later, the news reached our township: Nelson Mandela was now President Mandela, President of all South Africa.

The Ledger

VOTE ONE, VOTE ALL!
APRIL 27, 1994

SOUTH AFRICA'S FIRST OPEN ELECTION

Our President Mandela loved sports, and when South Africa was chosen to host the 1996 African Cup of Nations, he helped rally the whole country around our team.

On the rocky field in my township and on the grassy field in Johannesburg, we rooted for our team Bafana Bafana—"The Boys, The Boys."

I pretended to be John "Shoes" Moshoeu, the black midfielder.

"Shooooes!" I cheered when I booted the ball into the goal.

On his field, the blond boy pretended to be Mark Fish, the white defender.

"Feeeesh!" he cheered when he bicycle-kicked the ball between the posts.

In the opening match of the Cup of Nations, we watched Bafana Bafana thump Cameroon, 3–0. Then in the next round, we faced Algeria. Neither team could find the net in the driving rain, but midway through the second half, Mark Fish stormed past a defender and blasted a strike . . .

"Feeeesh!" We danced around the tiny television in town. "Feeeesh!"

Algeria fought back and tied the match, but with just five minutes remaining, Shoes Moshoeu rocketed a shot . . .

"Shooooes!" We poured into the street. "Shooooes!"

Bafana Bafana won again!

In the semifinals, neither Papa nor Mama believed Bafana Bafana had much of a shot against Ghana, the only undefeated team left in the tournament.

"You can't say we don't have a chance," my sister said. "Things are different now."

"It's a new day in South Africa," I agreed, repeating the words I'd heard at school and in church and on the bus and everywhere since the end of apartheid. "We can dream now. If Bafana Bafana wins, we must go to the finals."

"If Bafana Bafana finds a way to the finals," Papa said, "we'll find a way to the finals."

Bafana Bafana found a way!

Papa scraped together enough money for tickets, emptying change from the jars tucked behind the cupboard. When Papa finally purchased our tickets at the newsstand, I hugged him tighter than I ever had.

"Yebo, Bafana Bafana!" we cheered.

High in the packed upper deck of FNB Stadium, we chanted cheers and sang "Shosholoza" as Bafana Bafana took the pitch for the final showdown against Tunisia.

Standing on my seat, I spotted
the blond boy standing on his seat
in the next section.

He saw me and raised his fist.
I raised my fist back.

The tense match remained a scoreless duel
well into the second half.

50 minutes . . .

60 minutes . . .

70 minutes . . .

Suddenly, Mark Williams slipped past two
defenders and booted the ball toward Tunisia's net.

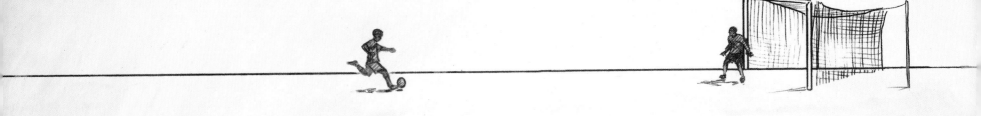

"Goooaaalll!"

Then, before we could sit back down, Bafana Bafana's amazing attacker broke free again and rocketed another ball toward Tunisia's side of the field.

"Goooaaalll!"

The final whistle blew. Bafana Bafana had won the African Cup of Nations!

Down on the pitch, the Bafana Bafana players paraded around, waving flags and blowing kisses.

The blond boy and I led the snaking line of frenzied fans in and out of the aisles and up and down the steps as we celebrated the first championship soccer trophy we'd ever won.

The next time I left the township,
I saw the boys playing on their field.

   "My name is Chris," the blond boy said,
trotting to the fence when he saw me.
"Do you want to play?"

   "Oh, yes!" I replied. "I'm Hector."

   He lifted the latch on the gate.
"When we play," he said, "I like to be
Mark Fish."

   "I like to be Shoes Moshoeu," I said.
"That means we're teammates."

   He opened the gate.

   I stepped through the soccer fence.

A LITTLE BIT OF HISTORY: When the South African national soccer team defeated Tunisia in the African Cup of Nations in 1996, they did much more than win a championship. They helped unite a divided country.

For centuries in South Africa, blacks were denied basic human rights, and in 1948, when the National Party took power, apartheid—the Afrikaans word for separation or apartness—became the official policy. Anyone who tried to resist apartheid was dealt with harshly. Anti-apartheid organizations, like the African National Congress, were banned, and many of their leaders, like Nelson Mandela, were sent to prison for life.

The global community objected to the South African government's racist policies. Throughout the 1970s and 1980s, individuals, companies and nations around the world boycotted South Africa. The international effort had a crippling effect on the South African economy and weakened the hard-line government.

At long last, apartheid began to crumble, and in 1990, President F. W. de Klerk announced the end of the policy. After twenty-seven long years in prison, Nelson Mandela was finally freed.

Still, the severely wounded country remained deeply divided. But sports played a major role in repairing the rift and healing the hurt.

Nelson Mandela loved sports. He understood they had the power to inspire and unite—they could play a pivotal role in bringing the country he loved closer together.

So a multiracial South African Football Association was formed, and a fresh national soccer team was born. On July 7, 1992, the first team to represent all South Africans played a match, and in a stunning upset, they defeated Cameroon. In an instant, a nation's spirits were lifted. Four years later, South Africa hosted the African Cup of Nations, and just as President Mandela had dreamed, children like the ones in *The Soccer Fence* and an entire country came together and rallied around a team.

For generations, apartheid crushed the hopes and spirits of black South Africans. But when Bafana Bafana went on their historic and improbable run, those thirty million blacks—and a reborn nation—found a reason to believe.

ACKNOWLEDGMENTS: Thank you to Elizabeth Becky Huffman, Keith Jacobson and Nonhlanhla Kheswa for sharing your experiences and for your valuable insights. Thanks to Khalil Anthony, Eva Ruiz and Orlando Reece for being bridges. And thanks to the Brooklyn Public Library. I'm so fortunate to have such a grand treasure walking distance from my doorstep.

SOURCES

BOOKS:

Clark, Nancy L., and William H. Worger. *South Africa: The Rise and Fall of Apartheid*. 2nd Ed. Harlow, England: Longman, 2011.

Malan, Rian. *My Traitor's Heart: A South African Exile Returns to Face His Country, His Tribe, and His Conscience*. New York: Grove Press, 2000.

Mandela, Nelson. *Long Walk to Freedom: The Autobiography of Nelson Mandela*. New York: Back Bay Books, 1995.

Mathabane, Mark. *Kaffir Boy: The True Story of a Black Youth's Coming of Age in Apartheid South Africa*. New York: Free Press, 1998.

Sonneborn, Liz. *The End of Apartheid in South Africa*. New York: Chelsea House Publishers, 2010.

Thompson, Leonard. *A History of South Africa*. 3rd Ed. New Haven: Yale University Press, 2001.

Tutu, Desmond. *No Future Without Forgiveness*. New York: Image, 2000.

INTERNET:

Nelson Mandela Centre of Memory: www.nelsonmandela.org

Apartheid Museum: www.apartheidmuseum.org

Time for Kids South Africa Timeline: www.timeforkids.com/destination/south-africa/history-timeline

Articles about South African soccer history:

www.abc.net.au/news/2010-07-08/seeds-for-success-sown-14-years-ago/897744

news.bbc.co.uk/sport2/hi/football/africa/8643962.stm

sportsillustrated.cnn.com/vault/article/magazine/MAG1143996/index.htm

The BBC Archive, which contains a rich collection of original news broadcasts, slideshows, interviews and documents, was an invaluable information destination: www.bbc.co.uk/archive/apartheid

FILMS:

Have You Heard From Johannesburg? (2010)

Endgame (2009)

Apartheid Timeline

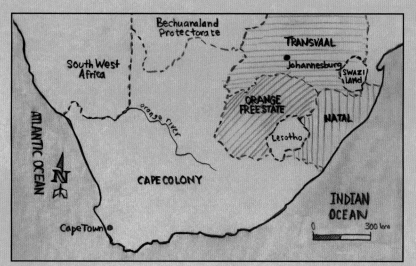

1910: THE UNION OF SOUTH AFRICA IS FORMED, comprised of four provinces—the Boer (Dutch) republics of Transvaal and Orange Free State and the British colonies of Natal and Cape Colony. Racial segregation becomes the official policy throughout the Union and lays the foundation for apartheid.

1912: The Native National Congress is formed to organize Africans in the struggle for civil rights. A few years later, it is renamed the African National Congress (ANC).

1913: The Natives Land Act, one of the first formal acts of segregation in the Union of South Africa, prohibits black Africans from owning land outside their region.

1944: Nelson Mandela joins the ANC.

1948: The National Party takes power. Apartheid is introduced.

1950s: A series of apartheid laws are enacted.

1950: The Population Registration Act classifies South Africans into three racial groups: white, colored (mixed race or Asian) and native (African/black).

1950: The Group Areas Act divides the country into geographic areas, each set aside for use by a separate racial category.

1951: The Bantu Authorities Act is the first piece of legislation supporting the government's policy of separate development.

1952: The African National Congress begins a Campaign of Defiance Against Unjust Laws.

1952: The Pass Laws Act requires all blacks over the age of sixteen to carry identification pass books at all times within white areas.

1953: The Reservation of Separate Amenities Act establishes "separate but not necessarily equal" parks, beaches, post offices and other public places for whites and non-whites.

1953: The Bantu Education Act racially segregates educational facilities.

1955: Different groups from the anti-apartheid movement come together to form the Congress Alliance and start the Congress of the People Campaign. Their demands are listed in the Freedom Charter. Their work mobilizes people and helps revive the ANC.

1957: South Africa is banned from the African Cup of Nations for refusing to field a multiracial team.

1959: Promotion of Bantu Self-Government Act: The reserves created in the 1913 Natives Land Act become separate countries known as homelands or Bantustans. The forced relocation of blacks begins.

1960–1994: Over 3.5 million blacks are uprooted and forced to relocate to barren Bantustans.

1960: Authorities open fire on a crowd protesting the pass laws in Sharpeville. Sixty-nine people are killed and many more are wounded. The incident becomes known as the Sharpeville Massacre and marks a turning point in the anti-apartheid movement.

1961: The government declares South Africa to be an independent republic from the British Commonwealth. Nelson Mandela heads the ANC's new military wing, the Umkhonto we Sizwe.

1961: FIFA, the governing body of the World Cup, bans South Africa from competition.

1963–1964: Nelson Mandela is arrested for treason and sabotage. At the Rivonia Trial, Mandela and seven other ANC leaders are sentenced to life imprisonment on Robben Island.

1966: The United Nations condemns apartheid as a crime against humanity.

1968: Stephen Biko establishes the South Africa Students' Organization, an all-black student group, promoting the Black Consciousness Movement.

1974: The United Nations votes to expel South Africa.

1976: Students at a Soweto high school riot and demonstrate against the apartheid educational system. Hundreds of people are killed and thousands are injured and arrested.

The incident becomes known as the Soweto Uprising and marks another major turning point in the anti-apartheid movement.

1977: Stephen Biko is killed while in police custody, further galvanizing the anti-apartheid movement.

1980s: People and governments around the world launch an international campaign to boycott South Africa.

1989: P. W. Botha, the hard-line president of South Africa, suffers a stroke and is forced to resign. His replacement, F. W. de Klerk, quickly realizes the only way forward is to release Nelson Mandela and unban the ANC.

1991: De Klerk repeals the remaining apartheid laws. Multiparty talks begin at the Convention for a Democratic South Africa (CODESA).

1993: De Klerk and Mandela are jointly awarded the Nobel Peace Prize.

1993: A multiracial, multiparty transitional government is approved.

1994: Nelson Mandela is elected president. The ANC wins sixty-three percent of the vote. The Government of National Unity is formed.

1995: South Africa hosts and wins the World Cup rugby tournament.

1994–1996: South Africa's first fully democratic parliament draws up South Africa's new constitution.

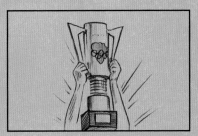

1996: BAFANA BAFANA wins the African Cup of Nations.

1996–1998: Truth and Reconciliation Commission hearings are held. Chaired by Archbishop Desmond Tutu, the hearings aim to promote reconciliation and forgiveness among the perpetrators and victims of apartheid.

1999: Nelson Mandela steps down after one term as president of South Africa. Thabo Mbeki is elected president.

2004: Nelson Mandela retires at age 85 and is granted the Freedom of the City of Johannesburg, the city's highest recognition.

2010: South Africa hosts the FIFA World Cup soccer tournament.

1990: NELSON MANDELA IS FREED FROM PRISON.
President de Klerk announces the end of apartheid.